# Sun Boiled Onions

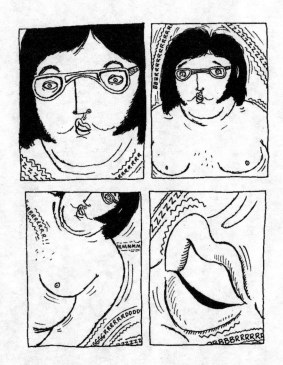

elvis

vic Reeves

MICHAEL JOSEPH
Published by the Penguin Group
Penguin Books Ltd, 27 Wrights Lane, London W8 5TZ, England
Penguin Putnam Inc., 375 Hudson Street, New York, New York 10014, USA
Penguin Books Australia Ltd, Ringwood, Victoria, Australia
Penguin Books Canada Ltd, 10 Alcorn Avenue, Toronto, Ontario, Canada M4V 3B2
Penguin Books (NZ) Ltd, Private Bag 102902, NSMC, Auckland, New Zealand

Penguin Books Ltd, Registered Offices: Harmondsworth, Middlesex, England

First published 1999
10 9 8 7 6 5 4 3 2 1

Copyright © Vic Reeves, 1999
The moral right of the author has been asserted

Set in Mrs Eaves
Designed in QuarkXpress on an Apple Macintosh by Smith & Gilmour
Printed in Great Britain by Butler & Tanner Ltd, Frome and London

A CIP catalogue record for this book is available from the British Library
ISBN 0–718–14396–5

# Sun Boiled Onions
## Vic Reeves

MICHAEL JOSEPH
LONDON

# FIN DE SIÉCLE
## or
# JOURNALE AU PAN MORTE

## Jan 1

Hoorah! The New Year has finally arrived.
I awake at 5 a.m. to find that a flock of seven
white doves of peace has flown in through the
bedroom window and begun to fly around
the room in formation in a kind of 'flight
of harmony', casting a Disneylike sense of
well-being about. Finally they roost on my
bust of Caligula and in the dim 1/8 light I'm
sure I saw one of them wink at me, a sort of
'wink of peace'. I take this to be an omen or
a sign of good fortune in the forthcoming
year and fall back to sleep.

I re-awake at 8 a.m. to find that the doves have
flown off with my bust of Caligula. Presumably
they have carried it off to their mountain eerie;
a foreboding sense of gloom now hangs over
the home.

I rise and decide to design a new type of hat. The place of work I choose this morning is underneath the bath, a safe place if any. My designs are at first sketchy, looking more like a fat young boy than a hat, but by 6 p.m. my design is complete and ready to be sent to Dunns & Co. for approval. I hope they like it. I think it would suit a more formal gentleman like a king or Harrison Ford. Here it is:

FACT

Elvis Presleys glossy
hair was grown by
himself.

Michael Jackson the King of Pop
had his head redesigned by a
porcelaine monkey on the crest
of mount Ararat and then floated
back down to earth having his
innards removed and pickled in
jars of frogspawn.
His chin had a packet of 20 silk cut
inserted into it and the fags
recieved via a draw under his
tongue. His nose insides were dug
out with a bent teaspoon and
replaced with a row of 'cheeses'
from his trivial persuit game and
a couple of orange tic tacs, his
hair replaced by fossilised leeches,
his lips, 2 redcurrants and his
eyes a pair of pifco lightbulbs.
Good luck to him.

4

MICHAEL
(Jackson)

Heard the new band Kokonut
Its white reggae played by
2 nice handsome lads from
Dudley and a big apelike
Simpleton retard farmer on
vocals.

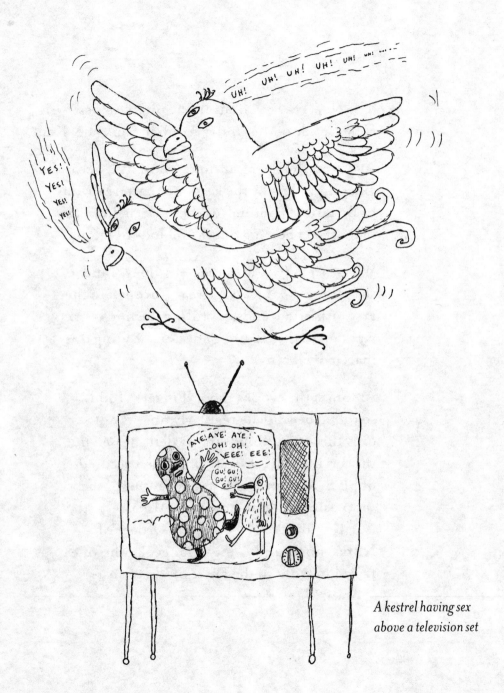

*A kestrel having sex
above a television set*

Jan 2

The New Year celebrations begin in earnest with
'The Parade of the Underworld' in Sandgate, Kent.

At 8 a.m. the sleepy antique-shop-filled seaside
village is woken by the kazoos and snare drums
of Britain's Criminals as they march down the
main street beating out the melody of felony.

What a sight it is, with the petty thieves and
shoplifters taking up the rear, through to the
arsonists and fraudsters filling the mid-ranks,
right up to the leading gangsters heading this
march of villainy.

Amongst the crooks I spot 'Fingers' Todd,
so called because he regularly fingers not
only the various foods in the delicatessen but
the serving ladies as well, and when accused
of his behaviour he blasts his way out of the
shop using a 75mm howitzer. Also present
is '2 Biscuits' MacDougal, the Grocer of
Kilmarnock, and 'Westy' Hancock, who once
farted in front of the Duke of Westminster
at point blank range.

Suddenly there is movement: one of the criminals breaks free from a mid-ranking group of builders and tries to flee in the direction of the sea, presumably to swim to France and freedom, but he is shot before he reaches the pavement by Jimmy 'Pineapple Caravan' Boyd from West Wittering.

And as the Underworld Parade vanishes into a hotel for their annual villains' breakfast of fried eggs, I too vanish back home for my breakfast of boiled eggs.

I spend the rest of the day looking at my feet.

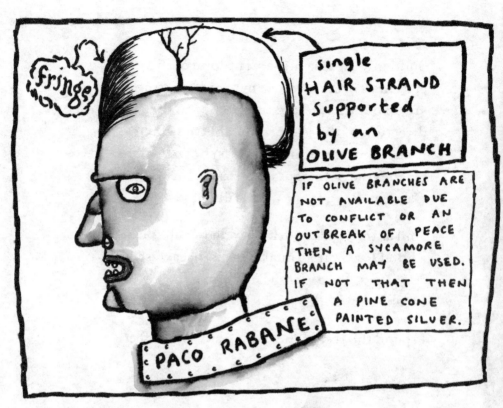

THE HAIRSTYLES OF SIX OF THE WORLDS TOP
PERFUMERERS AS THEY ATTEND A SECRET MEETING
ARE SHOWN ON THESE PAGES.

# Mike Givenchi

YOU SEE MIKE GIVENCHI'S MOUSTACHE?
WELL FROM THE FRONT IT LOOKS
LIKE A COMMON OR GARDEN 'HITLER'
STYLE, BUT AS HE TURNS TO FACE
THE DOOR YOU CAN'T HELP BUT
NOTICE IT STANDS OUT 6 INCHES
FROM HIS FACE!!

Morrissey the singer is seen here
thinking about who to ring in order to
get his loose tiles replaced in his kitchen.
He may, in a few hours, try ringing
Talking Pages for assistance, in turn they
may recomend a tiling firm or in
a few hours more he may decide to replace
them himself, days later he will drive to
Tile Kingdom in Hulme but sadly it will be closed
as it is Bank Holiday so he will replace them with
                                              cardboard.

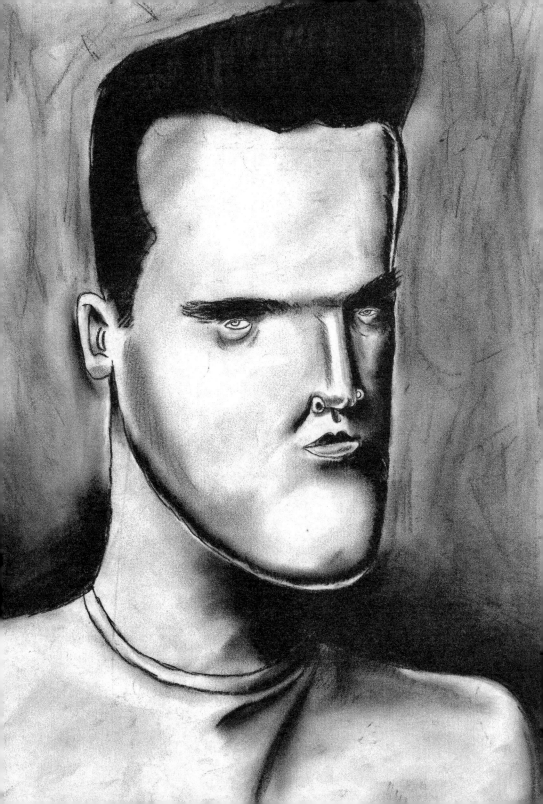

*A shrimp in a suitcase on a window ledge*

## Jan 3

I have had some thoughts on the possibilities
of opening new enterprises in the district,
for example (ie):

A) A combination asylum and pot-pourri centre
where the inmates create bags of pot-pourri to
allow your cabinets to smell sweetly, it shall be
called 'Scenti Mental'.

B) A series of old people's homes:
    1) Yesterday's People,
    2) Forgotten Faces,
    3) Time's Up,
    4) Conclusions.
A feature within the homes would be a dating
agency for old people called 'Expiry Dates'.

C) Health farms:
    1) Bye Bye Bulk,
    2) Fit & Farty.

I have sent off a number of ideas to the government in a bid to aid world peace. These products

are presented in advertisement form to aid the politicians to understand them and realize their true potential for global and universal harmony.

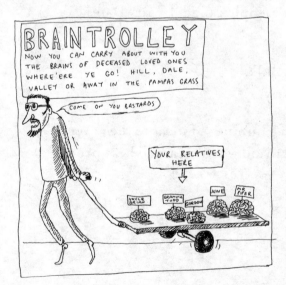

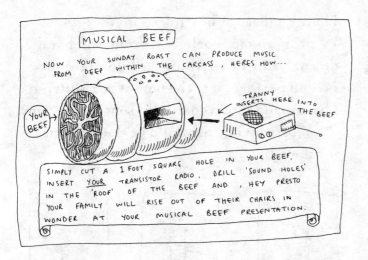

I have an idea for how to get on *New Faces*
TV programme. I believe it would win hands
down. Unfortunately for me I don't think
I could perform it to the best of its ability, so
I have made a storyboard and sent it to Jeremy
Paxman, who I think would be the ideal man
for the job.

CHAIR CHAMP

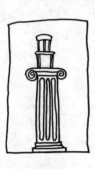

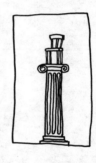

UUUUHHH!

UUGGNHHHH!!

BLEEAAARGHH!!

UUUGHA! UUUGHA!!

LAMOODOUURRR!!!

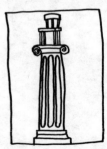

Its Sir Ronnie Corbett, you know
the guy who sits in the chair
and gives his opinions.
Anagram: RENT NICE ROBOT which
is what he done and named it
Ronnie Barker. success.

As the lights rose in the theatre
the audience realised that Elvis
had a spinal irregularity.

This gibb had the loveliest smile
on earth and put it to good use
in Newsagents and Jewellers as well
as Dixons and Holland and Barrett.
His award winning smile guaranteed
him free items in the shops as
well as free entry into Book Clubs
and Video Rental stores. His luxury
beam assured him of Freemans
catalogues gratis.

This guy plays so fast
he set his hand on fire
during a U.N. peace concert.
Thank god for the U.N.
fire extinguishing service, his
fire was doused and peace
was restored once again to
a troubled world. The guitarist
was arrested for halting the
peace process and burnt at
the stake.

Journey into

The journey into the
past can be a long
and arduous one.
The backbreaking
burden of such a trip
can tax even the
hardiest of men
often a painful
and revealing voyage
broken only by
occasional brief respites
of onanism.

the                    past!

## Jan 4

I awake to find thousand upon thousand
of tiny baby snakes on my head, but after
further investigation find that it is merely
my hair, which disappoints me tremendously,
although the thought of charming the baby
snakes into new and exciting hairstyles with
a flute thrills me. Never mind, I have recently
discovered a new snake in my trousers,
which seems to react to kindness and,
equally, threats!

## Jan 5

A crippled man came to my booth.

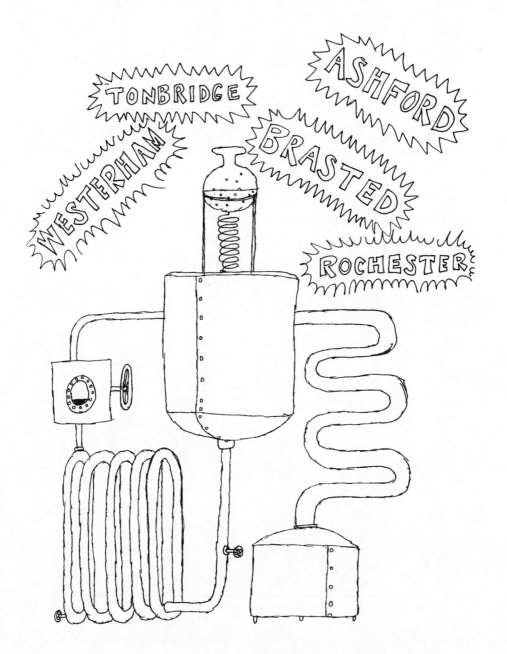

TONBRIDGE

ASHFORD

WESTERHAM

BRASTED

ROCHESTER

*An elaborate heating system apparently in Kent*

Elvis' first movie was
'My little pelvis' in which
he played a garage attendant
with a rotating hip region
enabling him to service
2 at once.

Jerry Halliwell, the spice dinner lady relaxes by having her hairs counted by subservient matadors who clamour for her attention. In return she offers them tales of sexual experimentation both on the high seas and on railway property. Her yarns can last up to 3 months therefore the spaniards invariably turn up with sandwiches

# Jan 6

Hey now! What's all this stuff in my bed!? I'll
tell you what it is, it's that old stuff, that old
biblical stuff, frankinsence. But how did it get
there? Let's examine the evidence . . . Last
night a crippled man invited me to a party
being held in his honour.

Who was this man? He looked like Patrick Swayze.

How was he crippled? When a flock of gulls,
excited at the arrival of the herring vessel, flew
into his legs, rendering them fairly useless in
cold weather.

What type of dancing was on offer? Mainly
Pavanes, but occasional Jitterbugging and that,
were available.

So where did this frankinsence come from then?
What! Wait a minute, this isn't frankinsence, it's
flaky skin! My flaky skin. Now I remember, on
the way home from the cripples' party I stared
into a workman's brazier until I had become
mesmerized by its luminous embers. As I gazed,
one of them leapt from its blistering bed like a

32

winged ingot on to my cool, cool lapel and lit it. Swiftly all my garments were ablaze and I leapt and vaulted, as one does when one is alight. I presented the night with an incandescent dance, illuminating the streets with my radiant shape, until a man dressed as Elizabeth the First extinguished me and I continued my night stroll home, pausing only for bread at a late-night supermarket. On arrival at the home I undressed and slipped silently between the sheets, gently smouldering. And so, this morning, as I rose, I discovered what I had initially interpreted as biblical frankinsence has turned out to be dry, burnt, flaked skin.

The power of recollection once again solved another morning mystery.

 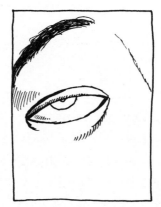 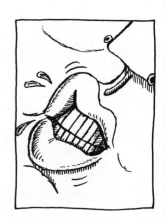

Terry-Thomas
was the first
man in space.

# Jan 7

I realized mid-morning that my bones had emerged through my fingers. The doctor tells me this is quite normal and I should in future refer to them as 'fingernails'.

If you ever suffer from these 'fingernails', here's a handy illustration for reference.

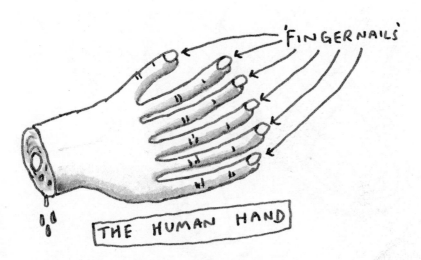

'FINGERNAILS'

THE HUMAN HAND

*A pair of tartan slippers*
*underneath a hedge*

## Jan 8

I found C&W star Waylon Jennings in my pear
tree. When I confronted him with my javelin
in hand he tried to hide behind a King
William, so I flushed him out with my
personal hose.

He wept and told me his woeful story of a Wild
West type family who lived near by and had no
'vittles' nor money due to their sweetcorn
crop failing, as they had recently suffered the
bitterest winter in near on forty years and
their steers had all been rooted out and stolen
by bad men and greedy landowners, so he had
to steal pears, so as they could 'jest git by'.

His tears fell like caustic rain on the dry, dry
earth and yet, somehow, I knew he was a-lyin',
so I shot him right there, in the pear tree.

At dawn I ring the police and tell them that I have mercilessly shot the rebellious Nashville singer Waylon Jennings and his undisturbed corpse is lying cold and motionless beneath the pear tree with robins circling overhead.

Twelve hours later the police strolled up to my door and asked to see the cadaver. I led them through the house and down the garden past the ornament to the pear tree. JESUS CHRIST OF BETHLEHEM!! The carcass had gone. I explained that the robins must have devoured him and suggested they keep their eyes open for a flock of robins with more red on their chests than normal.

They left silently and I cooked some of my secret recipe Wild West pork.

# JAN 10

Flies swarm around the pork in my attic,
so I get rid of it, all 150 lbs of it, in a ditch
near B&Q.

BENNY    ANGELA    ALFRED    B JORN

THE       ABBA

The Abba come from Norway.
They were brewed in a mystery
Ffyyorrdd by the explorer
Amundsen in a bid to finally
destroy the guns of Navarone.
On realising their lack of
potential as valid weapons to
strike at the heart of the 3rd Reich
they were bought by Dr Scholl footwear
~~manufacturers~~ and taught how to sing
music. They became The Netherlands
biggest export bar bacon and
sang a number of songs.
They blew up in 1982, Forty
years too late. The only survivor
was Benny as his nose was too
high to ignite the neutrons, ~~and~~
~~going~~

Here is the terrible day that Hank Marvin
contracted Ear warts by sleeping on a toad.
Cliff Richard on noticing them during the recording
of a hit sacked him from himself as earwarts
did not coincide with his christian beliefs and
were considered to be The Devils work Hank
left with the others leaving cliff alone to persue
his work. The others Welsh, Harris and Meehan
had also contracted Devils Poxes such as 'Night Globes'
'Valkyries' 'Eye Honey' and, in Welsh's case long
hornlike growths from his eyebrows with hands
on the end which created dark shadows beneath
onto his face which is where the shadows got
their name from.

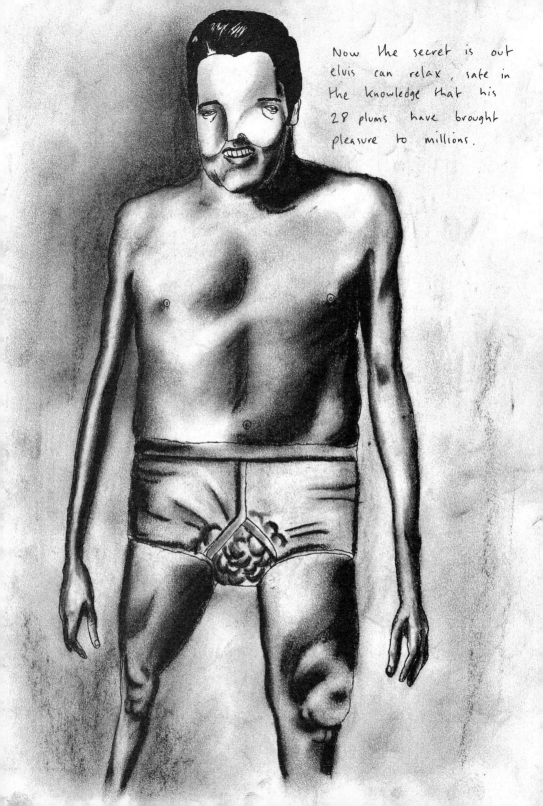

Now the secret is out
elvis can relax, safe in
the knowledge that his
28 plums have brought
pleasure to millions.

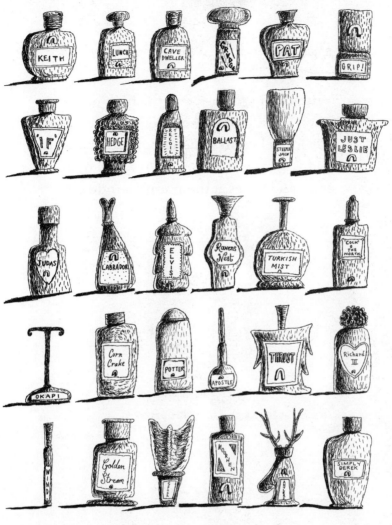

# FRAGRANCES BY 'Midnight Odours'

'You gotta smell sweet on a date, you gotta make
her know your the sweetest smellin' guy on the block
so go out now, throw your wallet on the counter
at the drugstore, demand a bottle of sweet smellin'
juice and tip the over you, guaranteed you'll be
humpin' by honniker.

## JAN 11

I attend a pageant where the high point was
when the Krankies were airlifted by an RN
Wessex helicopter and deposited in a tar pit
and visitors were then encouraged to hurl
coals and cokes at them until sundown.

A SARDINE SHRIMP IN A HAIRNET STARING AT A *PRIEST*

# WATCH OUT CHUM!
# ELVIS IS A GOOD FIGHTER.

Should you ever find yourself in the unrecommended
position of entering into a fight with Elvis the Pelvis
then beware, his punches can damage your tubes.
His skills were learnt from Cassius Clay the
world champion and his victory cry can
deafen even the hardest of boxers

THE 'CANON' & 'BALL'

Here comes The Cannon and Ball
with their lovely wools. making
the nation warm, and their
carving stuff making us see
new things in sticks. they come
with lab equipment supplying us
with remedies and panaceas, they
come with their wallpapers, their
devices, gases, keepsakes and
their nutmeg medallions but most
of all they bring us LAUGHTER.

JAN 12

Woke at 6 and drank 2 gals orange juice.

Went down to the swamp to get my oats.

Weren't nuthin there save them goddam ants
with faces like puppies, so I ate some o' them
critters and laid my juice down in the swamp.

When the swamp cooled a little I decided
to dredge that mother and get rid o' them
dog-faced ants once and f'r all.

I started dredgin' with ma dredgin' fork,
come up with a couple a dozen a dem ol' ints.
Sturted kinda makin' lurve t'em, den I blew
ma screw wid curtin dooks.

Den night fell.

P.S. Today

This is the poster from a Hollywood
Blockbuster film about a secretive naturist
soundrecordist who tapes a fellow nudist
trumpeteer who then dies during the recording,
his death was caused by poison.
    The identity of the killer is revealed when
the sound recordist listens back to his tape
and the killer is heard mid performance
applying paraquat onto the trumpet mouthpiece
whilst his victim blinked.

CONSERVATIVE POSTER 1997

Re:
Up the Tories poster
please mrs Thatcher
can u put this up
in your cabinet like.

You will get more votes
like. and make U.K.
Better place like.
Also to win election
you could try Bombing
Labour H.Q. with dynamite
like. Also make me
Foreign Sec. I will
kick out the blackies
and give away free oil
like.

    Yours Faithully

~~████████~~ Tarzan x

*A scoutmaster at daybreak putting peanuts in his glove!*

# Jan 13

Stinking, filthy gravy everywhere with onions
in it, accompanied by dumplings featuring
bacon, cheap bacon. Dirty, misshapen
gammon dumplings. Although this scene
was cleansed by the beautiful music that
filled the air.

ELVIS AS WALTER RALEIGH IN KING LEAR.

On Elvis only ever trip to England he appeared at the National Theatre as Sir Walter Raleigh in King Lear stunning onlookers with his decision to play the part naked from the waist down.

3 brothers once suffered bad luck, one of the brothers was crippled and attempted a journey to the ~~south~~ North Pole, seconds before he arrived at his destination 2 polar bears attacked him and devoured him whole.

Brother 2 was a
sailor with His majesty's
Navy, seconds before
discovering a new
latitude he contracted
Sailors Pox VD, ~~and~~
lost his mind and
forgot where he was.

OR OF TRANSFIGURATION

ORS POX VD

RTY MEN WITH SEX WOMEN SEE HOW IT WORKS NOW

STAGE 2 II

LUE FACE. KNACKERS DISOLVE.
EAR OF CHRIST THE SAVIOUR SON OF
OD THE CREATOR. CHICKENS. YOU WILL
ECOME DAFT. SEMEN FEAR. NEGATIVE
ARS. MIND CALOUS. DEEP QUEERNESS

STAGE 3

YELLOW FATIGUE. COYNESS. DIRT
GOD AS ENEMY. CHRIST WITH JOWLS.
LOVE ONLY FOR HERRINGS. KILLER MENTALITY
EARS TURN INTO HAMMERS. CHINESENESS.

Those Terrible ANTS have done it again whilst I slept but this time they have tak my AR and my wo has not yet bee complete ......

I AM CURSED

SORROW
RAGE
The necklace
FURY AT ANTS
of Ant Bitterness
TERROR
HATE

white Ants

The third brother (3) was a genius at Tapestry
and seconds before completing a vast complex tapestry
ants got into his workplace and ate his arm.

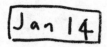

EGG DAY (more faces came). Egg day was
spoilt once again by the faces that have been
coming.

WHAT ABOUT THIS HAT!!?

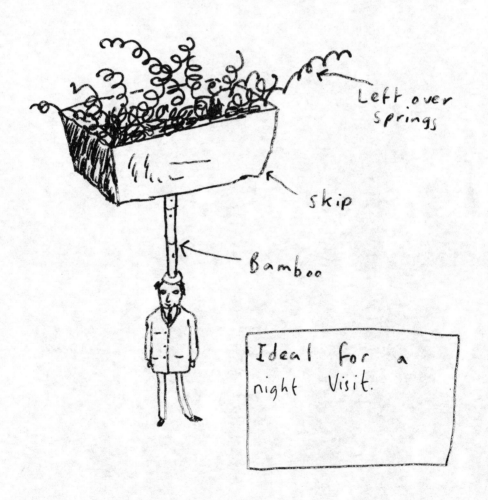

Left over
springs

skip

Bamboo

Ideal for a
night visit.

Do you remember the Bubonic Plague or
'BLACK DEATH'? Well, it came from RATS!
Remembering this fact, I grew wary of a rat I
discovered in my Ricicles and examined it
with my eyeglass as it gently lapped up the milk
that held the Ricicles in semi-suspension. I
noticed that the rat was smooth, with a large,
oval head and a thin, tapered body.

After a few hours' examination I grabbed the
rat, withdrew it from my now soggy Ricicles
and hurled it out of the window on to the
midden, where it lay dormant and silent,
never moving again.

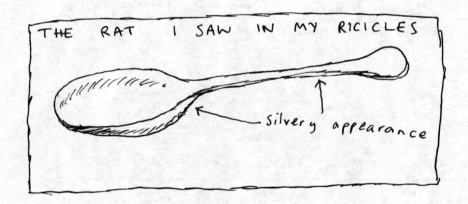

THE RAT I SAW IN MY RICICLES

Silvery appearance

Henry the 8, No 8 King in G.B. had
his 7 wives killed by the following
methods :-

Anne of cheese — De headed by firemans axe.
Ann Blin — De frosted
Mary queen of scots — Dinamite
Jane Mansfield — Red hot poker
Jane Seemore — grassy knoll
Q.E.1 — Motorway bridge
Lucrecia Borge — Cromwell garden style

*A Tudor vacuum cleaner*
*saying 'How do you do?'*

Elvis and Frank were on their way
to the Argos shop one day for a
fan heater quietly discussing their
plans for the ideal location to place
it for maximum heat distribution in
their flat and also the delicate
subject of sharing said heater when
they were disturbed by a gurgling
rattling sound behind them. They turned
simultaniously and looked to see directly
behind them their old friend Sammy Davis Jr
choking on tube of pritt stick he had
been using to glue his glass eye back in.

ELVIS & FRANK ON THEIR WAY TO THE SHOPS

The Jimi Hendrix Experience were the first All Black rock band being all Afro American except Mitch Mitchell and Noel Redding.

Their hits included 'The wind cries mary' written after Jimi broke wind and the subsequent anal voice (fart) appeared to say 'Mary' in a high pitched farty way.

Jimi was known to occassionaly gnaw at his guitar if no peanuts were available, his flambouyant gestures and shirts often startled people into thinking he was a peacock and throwing him peanuts.

The other two were drab in comparison and when Jimi sadly died in 1970, mitch went back to being the monkey in supercar and Noel a DJ and host of House party.

Look out, its Eric Morecambe
and he's in a bad mood, run
back to your house, unlock
the padlock on your front
door and hide, hide anywhere
you can for Eric is fuming
and its you he's after, with
his black glove, he's gonna
do ya!

As Elvis relaxed at the rodeo watching the horses
doing it in the paddock he almost forgot about
his back nodules with their tiny radar hairs.
That was until Frank Sinatra crept up and
pinched a fiver out Elvis' back winnings pocket.
Elvis was dissappointed that his friend could do
such a thing where as Frank couldnt care
less and spent the money on some Italian stuff.

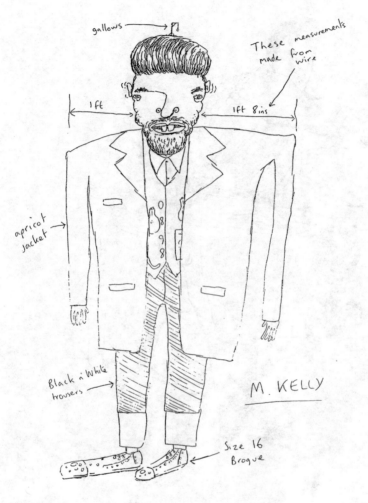

gallows →

These measurements made from wire

1ft

1ft 8ins

apricot jacket →

M. KELLY

Black n' White trousers →

Size 16 Brogue

Its Matthew Kelly with his dimensions. Just before he goes on his Stars in Eyes programme he shows these dimensions to his butler who then makes him fit.

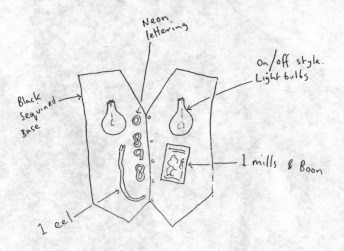

Neon. lettering

On/off style. Light bulbs

Black Sequined Base

1 mills & Boon

1 eel

# M. KELLYS
## WAISTCOAT

M. Kellys waistcoat
features.
The lightbulbs represent
the eyes of god.
The Neon Lettering
represent the gift of
0898
The Eel represents
movement through
drainage ditches
and the Mills and
Boon represents
knowledge.

If ELVIS the pelvis was a miner then
this is ~~what~~ how he would have appeared
to the other members of the parish as he
strode manfully from his pit on the mountainside
clutching whats left of his filthy pasty and
cherryade bottle, his face blackened by
coal juice and his singing voice gravelly
and raw just as Bonnie Tylers was as
she emerged from her welsh colliery, lungs
filled with smuts.

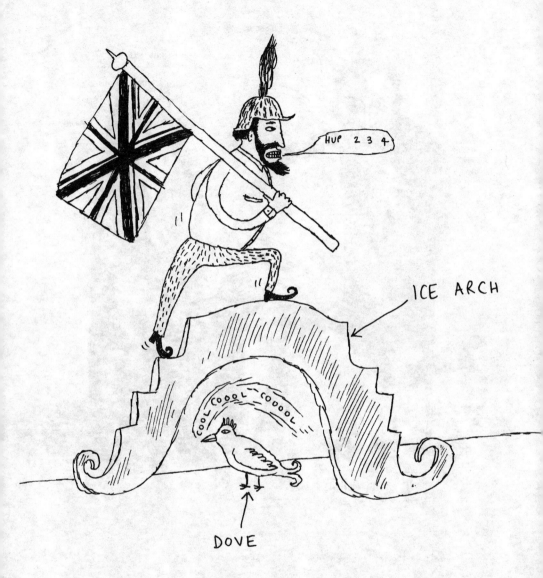

*A specially formed ice arch*
*for climbing over doves*

Jools Holland with his ivory fingers
pestering his keyboards into delivering
hoochie koochie music to the nation.
His wry smile and dirty hair
filled with ointments. Snakeskin boots.

## JAN 16

A man came by early this morning about 4.30 a.m. with a little cart and asked me if I would like to go for a ride in it. He was a rather sinister-looking, red-faced, portly man with one white eye. His filthy Arran sweater was filled with holes and his slacks were black with oil and grease.

I jumped in and off he pulled me in his little dog cart, bouncing over the rocks and potholes at a fair lick for about 15 miles, when there, over the brow of a hill, we saw a walled city. At the city gates he spoke quietly and secretively to a guard, who then let us in through a small workmen's gate. He paid the guard and we entered the city and he pulled me through the throngs of traders in the market square to his stall. On arriving, it was then quite apparent that the man intended to sell me for *meat*.

'I am N O T meat,' I said characterfully to the man.

'Then why,' said he, 'did you not tell me this at 4.30 a.m.?'

THE DIRTY MAN WHO THOUGHT I WAS MEAT AND TOOK ME TO THE CITY IN HIS LITTLE CART.

'Because,' I wearily stated, 'at 4.30 a.m. I had
no idea you intended me for meat. At 4.30 a.m.,
when you asked me to ride in your cart, I thought
you had come to collect me to take me to the
magistrates' court, where I am currently in the
middle of prosecuting a rat that trespassed in
my Ricicles, you one-eyed shit!'

And so the man turned around and pulled
me back home, but to show there were no hard
feelings, and feeling sorry for him having no
meat to sell, I gave him the rat that I had thrown
on to the midden. 'Here,' I said in a gentle voice,
like Jesus Christ, 'here is your meat to sell at
market today. Take it with my best wishes and
return to your stall and sell it.'

'Thank you,' said the man, and he put the rat
in his little cart and turned around and went
off back to market. I patted myself on the back
and congratulated myself at being such a kind
and considerate person and rewarded myself
with a large bowl of onion soup. But to my
horror and repulsion another rat had crept
into my bowl of soup.

The scourge of the good and kind!
The sight that strikes fear into
the hearts of descent men.
The terrible evil, the unspeakable
invention that causes worldwide
misery to agreeable people.
Making honourable hard working
folk run for cover, fleeing
in despair from the dreadful
item. The sooner the U.N.
realise this and remove it once
and for all from the hands of
rotten men ~~the sooner better~~ and replace
it with cotton wool the better.

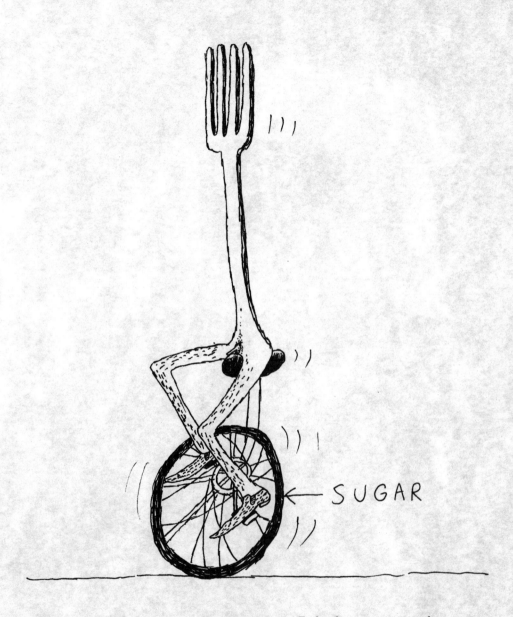

SUGAR

*Fork riding a sugar unicycle*

One dark sleepless night elvis prowled his
flat and caught a glympse of himself
in the mirror and out of the inky gloom
he noticed his chin had grown to some
extent.

Andy Warhol is seen here in a wind tunnel having a force 12 blown at him to see if his wig will fly off if he visits chicago, the windy city.

Thank goodness it remained otherwise it would have had to have been nailed on which could potentially have caused malfuctioning.

VIC REEVES

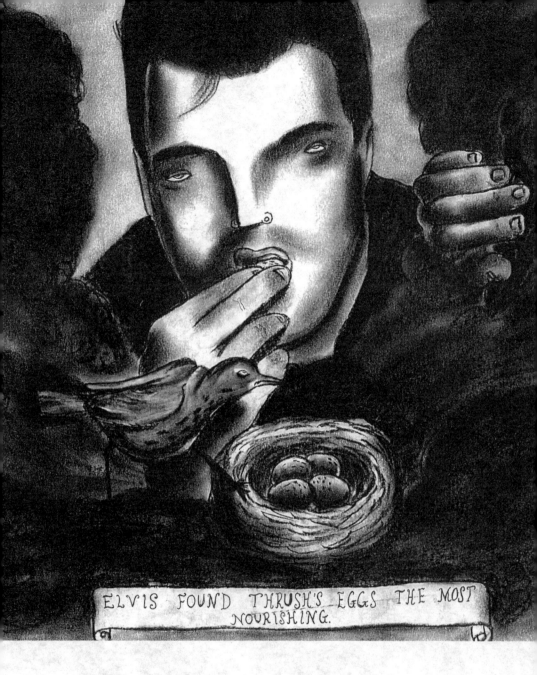

ELVIS FOUND THRUSH'S EGGS THE MOST NOURISHING.

When Elvis was stranded on the Island he survived the 15 years he spent there on eggs and the oil from cods.

I awoke and heard cockneys downstairs.
I hid behind the door and heard them talking
in the living room, then one of them let out a
blood-curdling scream. I ran in with my baton
to confront them. What a fool I felt: it was
'The Eastenders' on television. I apologized
to them and explained the situation, and after
20 minutes or so they went and were replaced
by Anne Robinson and Alice Beer.

I felt quite stupid, although the blood-
curdling scream had actually curdled my
blood and stopped it from travelling round
my body successfully, which was a bore, so
I composed a letter to the cast of 'The
Eastenders' informing them that I would
shortly be suing them for curdling my blood
and would be seeking compensation in the
form of money and a blood transfusion.

Paul Daniels is a conjurer, a sorcerer whose only tenet is to mystify and bewitch people with his wizardry. When they are succesfully under his command he leaves the arena and his subjects perplexed and confused as he runs down the streets cackling his impy laugh at their gullibility at falling for his ball and cup trick.

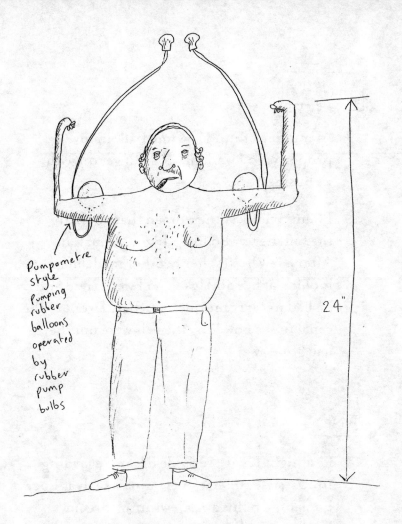

Pumpometre style pumping rubber balloons operated by rubber pump bulbs

24"

MICHAEL WINNER

M. Winner workout dummy. Now you can see what it looks like to notice M. Winner in your gym. in the privacy of your own toilet.

## JAN 18

At midday I found a 'Time Ball' in my
property, so I went out to let it get on with
its business.

I went to look at the woman that works in
the butcher's who looks like a Dalmatian.
After a few hours, her brother made me stop
looking at her and leave, so I went rigid and
he had to carry me out like a bar. I went to the
canal to see how long the eels were but they
had gone away.

## JAN 19

Last night I had a terrible dream regarding
1920s-style American criminals such as Lucky
Luciano. In this award-winning dream
Luciano, Dillinger, Pretty Boy Floyd and
Machine Gun Kelly came over to show off,
jumping around and waving their machine
guns in the air and shouting words like
'Buster' and 'I'm swell'.

And lo it was so that god descended from his celestial perch and came to earth and so it was. And lo he begat a unique sausage beside the 3 mountains of ararat, and he said unto all men, "Lo the sausage", and so it was and it was decreed and Lo the sausage begat a son and Lo this child begat a daughter and it was so. And God said 'It is good" and lo it was good and so it was. see!

Ralph
Vaughan
Williams 1

The composer Ralph Vaughan Williams with
his features is looking right into an olive
hole. although his hearing piece cannot detect
any sound he is pretty ~~dumb~~ sure it is silent
He's been staring into the olive for 3 hours
and has detected <u>NO</u> movement. Soon his
interest will wane and he will move to another
area where he will stare into a gun barrel.

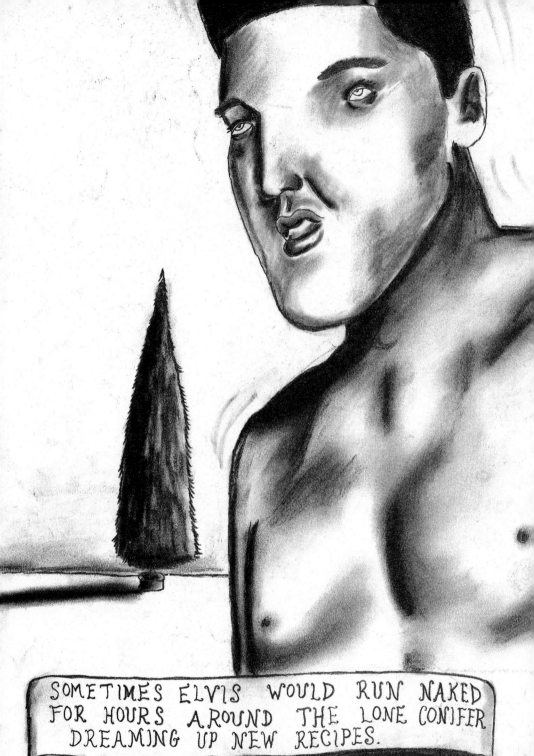

SOMETIMES ELVIS WOULD RUN NAKED
FOR HOURS AROUND THE LONE CONIFER
DREAMING UP NEW RECIPES.

VIC REEVES

# JAN 20

Today my house is surrounded by crows who,
I believe, want to murder me and take me away
to their evil master. Here are some of the
names I have given them:

Yeomen of Filth
The Hooded Sentinels of Satan's Gallery
Dirt Beagles
Filthy Couriers of the Grave
Bastards!

They came at noon and perched on my
shovels, wishing me ill with their persistent
'whore, whore, whore!', winking their black
button eyeballs at me and doing a kind of
Lindy hop on the shovels.

It is night now and I am relieved to discover it
isn't me they want but the carrion I have been
eating and discarding outside the house.

The Fab Four
Beatles with their
hairstyles based on mops
and their funereal suits
came from Liverpool, the
riviera of the North East.
Singer Ring 'O' so called
because of his 'o' shaped
ring was a deaf mute
whose father invented
the spoon.
All the group had
downward sloping eyes
giving them the impression
of four melancholic
chipmunks which they
were occasionally mistaken
for and caged by concerned
zoologists. They had
some hits.

THE

1959-

1937-

GEORGE HARRISON

RING 'O'

GUITAR

DRUMMER

# FAB 4

## (BEATLES)

1931 -

1941 - 80

'MACCA' McCARTNE

LENNON

GUITAR

GUITAR

BY JINGO! HOW ELVIS LOVES TO SURF

AMONGST THE STILL-LIFES.

*A lemon pip with sideboards*
*fighting a bearded crab*

DONALD SINDEN

Donald Sinden with is lovely voice as rich
as christmas cake gazes benignly from this
wonderful portrait as if to say, in his
virile, sonorous way. "Time for a glass of
sherry I believe" as he does so often to
the check out assistants at B & Q when he
is buying his screwdrivers.

I rose bright-eyed and filled with joy. I leapt
from my bunk and did my party trick into
a bucket full of dried wine, then danced so
violently I broke my arm. It turned out not to
be broken, simply trapped up the chimney.

After dislodging my arm, I grew fearful that
Rasputin was in the house, moving sideways
and eating chips, but I then realized it was
my reflection in the mirror.

I shaved and with the collected hairs I wove
a hammock to lie in and think things up.

I was visited at dusk by a man who suspended
two women wearing bow-ties. He was a very
handsome man, whom I first took to be James
Garner, but on closer inspection with my
magnifying glass he turned out to be simply
a handsome beggar with two huge women on
him. I shut the door on him, and when he at
last realized, some 3 hours later, that I had
not given him the time of day, he tried to
kick a number 2 through my letterbox.

The man suspending two
women wearing bow ties

TALLY HO! ELVIS LOVES
A NICE CUPPA AS HE
RIDES IN THE MOONLIGHT
ON HIS FAVOURITE REINDEER.
JESS.

VIC REEVES

like Mad King Ludwig
before him Elvis
rode famous journeys
distances in circles
on his reindeer.
When the journey was
completed Elvis shaved
and read cosmo until
his gyro arrived.

*Bono in a boob-tube*
*on a choirmaster's lap!*

Its Shane McGowan the
jug eared singer with his
bad face and teeth. Shane
has one tooth for every day
of the week and one spare
but no-one knows where it
grows.

When Charles Darwin made his discoveries
on his Beagle one thing was for sure...
'The Ascent of Man' was on its way!
He discovered that monkeys can turn into
men, that lizards never leave the
galapagos islands and that Koala bears
eat leaves, what is next for us here
on the lonely blue planet?, perhaps cops
will become buttery, maybe ice will dry
and Elvis re-emerge, as a swamp cat,
who knows but ~~thanks~~ fanx for the memories
Mr Darwin.

This urn contains the remains of Dick Turpin.
And a tomato, his final stolen object. Taken
from Lady Hamilton as she travelled in her
stagecoach through Nottingham forest on the
way to a party at Lord Nelsons house,
the tomato was going to be her gift
to him but sadly, following the theft,
all she had to offer him was some salt
sachets she nicked from a Happy Eater on the way.

Play the pipes of Pan sweet Elvis until the
mermaid appears once again in that bucket.
Guard him with your life body guard, let
no one stop him from making his sweet music
lest the merman shall not appear again
in the oil tank.

Eggs are laid by birds, right? So what's a dog
doing laying an egg in my churn? That's
right, a Labrador came into my vision this
morning clutching a dirty flannel between its
nicotine-stained, chipped teeth and strolled
straight up my path, bold as brass, winked at
me and laid a large white egg in my churn.
On closer inspection it was the postman,
and what I thought was a dirty flannel was his
beard, the egg a letter, although he is from
Labrador and has a tail, although it may just
be his postbag, come to think of it!

I opened the letter. It was from a woman
I knew 20 years ago. I met her at the circus
and attempted to conduct relations with
her behind the ape van.

'You're like an octopus,' she exclaimed with
raised eyebrows and mouth agape – not as you
may think because of my wandering hands,
but because I squirted ink at her when she
tried to prise me out of my crevice.

In her letter she requested the return of a packet of everton mints I had stolen from her cabin many, many years ago. She had spent the following years travelling the earth searching for me, encountering many varied adventures involving balding men, pineapples and grinding wheels, over deserts and ice floes, squalor and riches, until she discovered my whereabouts from a man in a tank and sent her letter. So I sent the mints back. They were off.

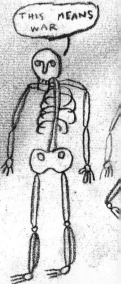

HORSE PEANUT

THE KRANKIES AIRLIFTING
MICKEY MOUSE OUT OF A
DUSTSTORM FULL OF
SKELETON.

When Mickey mouse lost
his way in the fields of
Pandemonium on the banks
of Hades caused by his
Helter Skelter downward
spiral Hollywood drink and
drug hell he plummeted into
the infernal regions hurled
into the abyss and for his
sins condemned to everlasting
torment until the krankies
airlifted him out and took
him for a fish and chip
supper in Weston Supermare

CHEGGERS

PERISH
THE
THOUGHT

*A Battenburg owned by Jesus that can miraculously talk*

HELLO ELVIS
WHOSE YOUR FRIEND?

When Elvis met Nixon
and shook in agreement
it was a good day for
all bar the stinking
Kmer Rouge.

ALBINO TONY BLACKBURN
whiter than bleach, hides
in drifts and leaps upon
passing men in his white
garments. When he has
attatched himself to them
they know not where he is
by sight, only by weight.

He rummages through their
pockets and pouches in search
of little silvery objects like
trinkets and 5p's and as
quick as he arrived, so he is
gone, back to his milky
hideaway to examine ~~count~~ his
cache.

114.

. Today I cooked my shoes.

Today is my birthday, so I celebrated the good news by soiling my underwear in a carefree manner, striking many differing poses as I did so: first this stance, now this shape, the concurring movements reaching the outer limits of bowel evacuation. I strode about triumphant and filled with dirty glee. Undergarment warfare. A blitzkrieg on besmirched boxers.

With a burnt-out bottom I went into the snow to carry out my work. It was chill under foot, the glistering particles melted beneath my hot feet, which now resembled burgers following my attack on them with a welding torch in the early hours. Having completed my work, I slammed the greenhouse door and all the glass fell out and into the pots containing the sultanas, so I spent the next seven hours picking it out and Sellotaping the glass back together and replacing it into the frames.

As evening fell, I decided I was tired of being blind, so I removed the fish kettle from my face and settled down to watch the TV (television). After an hour I turned it on but the images were too rapid and I was sick on my binoculars, so I had to walk all the way back to the TV and turn it off.

In order to cheer myself up I went to sleep.

Squalk, clash, schree, gack, smelt, clash! I heard above my chimney as I arose from my night bed. At first I thought it to be iron pans moving inside the chimney, but no, there was no kitchenware in that chimney today. 'I know what it will be,' I barked to myself. 'It must be the roof scratching its tiles together in an attempt to have a conversation with the sun or some other airborne globe or something else.'

I went outside to quantify my judgement only to see two eagles in an aerial battle to the death. The flight appeared to be over the ownership of a scratchcard that I noticed on the ground, either that or territory, who knows, anyway I let them get on with it and went back inside and had some Rice Crispies.

For to celebrate the birthday of his friend Richard Nixon, Elvis presented himself in a fascinating way at the presidents flat. When Mr Nixon openned the door he didnt recognise the King in his disguise and slammed the door in his face. Elvis reknocked and exposed himself. Nixon instantly recognised him and allowed him in.

The bloke out of The Beach Boys with the wide head.

I get around! Huhn!?

'I get around' sang the Beach Boys in
1932, but the bloke out of them
with the striped shirt misread the lyric
and got a round head by pumping
ox blood into his eyes giving him the
~~dis~~ appearance of a wide eyed moon.
Paul Daniels achieved this effect also
not as you may think by magic but by
the ~~nigko~~ly exersize of crushing his head
between ~~two~~ two hot ingots.

The fisherman returns
at dawn with his
catch and proudly
displays it to his
eager wife and child.
8 fish . 8 fine
sardines that they
shall cook that
evening for their
buffet tea held
in honour of
Neptune and
his bounteous
cornucopia that
allows the
fisherman and his
family to dine
each day on his
sweet sweet sardines

e fisherman and
his wife

The day the fisherman caught only one sardine the shame bore heavy upon his head, this shame took the form of a squirrel who leapt down and devoured the fish, the fisherman killed and ate the squirrel who had the fish in his belly and pride was restored to the fisherman. and his family

This morning at dawn a real Wild West
cowboy came to the house and sold me some
'Ass Balm', which is great for someone in my
position and I can highly recommend it to
racing-car drivers, office workers, traction-
engine operators and buggers alike.

CAPTAIN DEATHS ZOOMED OFF ON HIS NEW 'RACER' TO 'THE SWEETIE SHOP'.

"HELLO, MR. SWEETIE SELLER" HE CRIED "PLEASE MAY I HAVE 1 LB OF FRUIT PASTELS"

*A badger with an afro throwing
sparklers at the Pope!*

At 5.00pm he left his cottage
and strolled down the lane
to the shop where he would
like to buy his meal, on
his way a sinister visitor
asked him if he was going
to the shop. Elvis stopped
and looked at him and
the stranger looked back.
2 hours later Elvis stopped
looking at him and went
off to the shop. By this
stage it was 7.15 pm and
the shop had closed.
Elvis returned, the visitor
was still there so Elvis
kicked his head in and
went home.

HELLO ELVIS, ON YOUR WAY TO THE SHOPS THEN?

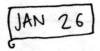
JAN 26

Went to get the bleach from the depot. I saw
lizards at war on the way. I covered my crotch
as I passed by, just in case they turned on me.

I filled the wheelbarrow with bleaches and
jogged back singing *Tannhäuser* and the song
of the whale, when I came across a stump, where
I relaxed for some time. Whilst I stood relaxing
by the stump, a young man came to look at me.
He wore a red, rubbery hat with five points and
had a goitre. He was dressed in the finest
bronze feathered cloak and had scrawny legs.
He pecked at the earth awhile then walked off
singing 'Rock and Boogaloo, Rock and
Boogaloo, Rock and Boogaloo' until he
disappeared into the bushes.

The next visitor was Jomo Kenyatta and
after him the singer Blondie with her backing
group, Blondie.

When I got home, I put the bleaches into the test tubes and stored them away in my secret labyrinth and settled down for dinner with Blondie. She had dismissed her backing group, Blondie, and returned with me in the bleach-barrow.

I spoon-fed her the sultanas, as she had no arms, nor legs for that matter. It was difficult to feed her as she had no mouth or face. I began to grow sceptical about her being Blondie and decided to check in my Encyclopedia of Rock. She looked nothing like her, she looked more like a brick. So I took her outside and threw her down the well. I should have invited Jomo Kenyatta instead, with his lovely black and yellow striped sweater.

Here come the Gallagher Brothers
from The Oasis. each hair within
their eyebrows representing an inner
emotion in conflict with their motions

8 shaped man woman
wearing her iron bonnet
doing her shape at
the U.N. in order to
bring peace to all nations.

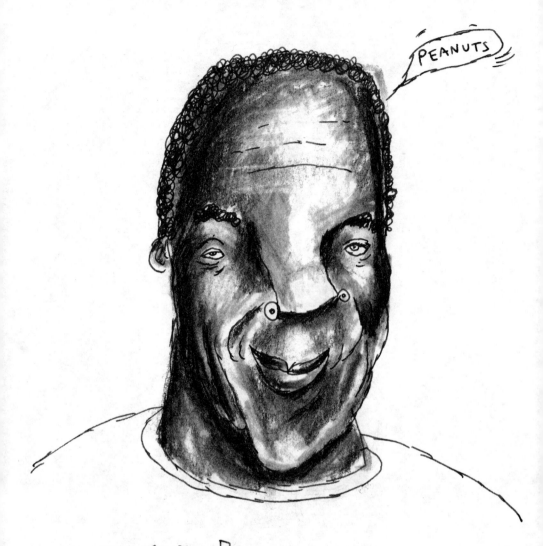

Yes, he's that american actor
who lives in Manchester Town Hall
and presents the Big Breakfast.
He has a trolley selling hot nuts
outside the arndale and helps
out in winter focusing tourists
cameras on pigeons.

As Elvis Ironed his slacks in
the cottage a a stranger looked
through his kitchen window at him
and asked him if he was enjoying
his time spent ironing his slacks.
Elvis stared at him for 4 hours
and then continued ironing. he had
to re-iron the slacks though as his
hands had gripped the slacks so
tightly over the 4 hour period he
caused more creases than they had
in them before.

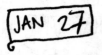

JAN 27

Last night I dreamt of Florence (Firenze), of
the cathedral in her majesty, of the wonderful
railway station, the pretty squares filled with
statues and the old bridge with its jewellery
shops selling their vulgar gold bracelets.

Will I ever return? I hope not; last time I was
there I was arrested for drilling holes in the
magnificent statue of Neptune. I was locked
up before I could put in the dowels which
would act as perches and offer a roost for eagles
and make the statue even more tremendous.

That's the thanks I got from the Italian
government: 3 years of solitude in a Tuscan
Barn, regularly sprayed and fed only on those
butter-beans. Still, my escape was daring.
After the keepers had gone to sleep in their
villa, I hid myself inside some electronic
equipment in the repair shop. The following
day I could hear the sirens and dogs from my
haven beneath the keypad. A week later the
electronic machinery was sent to Düsseldorf
to be repaired. I made good my escape whilst
a disabled Kraut boffin ate his cabbage in

the corner and fled the building disguised
as a man. I leapt on a railway train carriage
transporting cabbage to Berlin for the
festivities and gorged myself all the way.
Short of Berlin I hurled myself from the
carriage and hid in a cabbage field until
nightfall, when I made my way through the
cabbages to Stuttgart. In Stuttgart I became
a watchmaker of great repute until the
authorities discovered who and what I was
and I once again fled, this time to Geneva,
where my cravings got the better of me and
I began to drill holes in various statues around
the city. I was arrested and this time, to prevent
escape, I was confined in a glass sphere deep in
the heart of the lake and fed peanuts down an
elaborate piping system for 8 years, until one
morning I heard a tapping on my globe. It was
him, Neptune. He had heard of my plans to
attract eagles to his image and was delighted
with the plan and so freed me from my
submerged orb and we swam, oh how we swam,
through blue lagoons and deep dark trenches,
through seas filled with fire in Hawaii, beneath

ice packs and coral bays to the Sargasso Sea,
where I mated one final time and swam the long
journey home to Norfolk, where I remain to
this day in a lock along with the other eels,
waiting for the day we shall be free.

*A family of foxes glowering at some soap*

QUEEN ELIZABETH 1 URINATING IN THE STYLE OF A <u>MAN</u>.

That poor ghost tortoise was
passing by on the way to the
Klondyke gold rush in search of
a cure when Q.E.1. monarch
appeared on the roof and passed
onto this ghost tortoise hampering
him momentarily and leaving him
short sighted for a few seconds.
On the plus side. It was the cure!

WAKE UP ELVIS

Elvis was prone to drowsy periods where he daydreamed of Ice partridges on the banks of the Clyde, he dreamt of gutter snipes and sun boiled Onions, of Little mob caps dancing through bluebell encrusted pastry valleys until the reality of Heartbreak Hotel awoke him from his reverie and plunged him into another, this time melancholic torpor.

143

I know my life is coming to an end, I see
cavaliers at my window with their glorious hats
with feathers and their faces all a-covered in
bits of Blu-Tack. Never mind.

I keep going blind for short periods. I first
noticed this last week. It's almost as if for a
split second I am totally blind and then can
see again. Long ago this also happened —
the doctor said it was called 'Blin King'.

*A lump of Nazi nougat
walking down an avenue*

Had Elvis lived to an old age
then this is what he would
have looked like as he
entered the dining room of
the old peoples home.

MARTY CANE

Lovely Marty Cane
with her singing voice
and affectionate glint.

Crabsticks everywhere, with flies. In come
Navajo Indians with church-mice. It is so cold,
so bitterly cold here in this fridge . . . and
dark, pitch black and cold, and the racks have
made frozen marks on my nakedness, my eyes
have turned to marbles, I have chattered so
much that my teeth have fallen out.
The end is nigh.

Freedom is mine. I perished today.

DROWSY ELVIS

Sleep now sweet Elvis, and dream of
the sweet smelling Corn cob fields of your
native Kentucky. Drowse away your
worries and slumber peacefully in your
rhinestone encrusted 'jamas 'til dawn
brings new songs and karate chops[149]
to excite your public.

I have returned as a spectre and dance around
my house in a carefree manner moving
furniture and 'shooting the shit' with other
phantoms whom I have invited to dwell with
me in Purgatory. We dine on air and flit
rather than walk. Oh what peace there is in
the grave. Hoorah for transparency, huzzar
for apparitions, 3 cheers for the unearthly
world of ghouls, wraiths, banshees and
manes — for that is what I am now, you
can lay to that. I am a phantasm . . .

. . . I think